# The
# Storm
# Leopards

www.hollywebbanimalstories.com

STRIPES PUBLISHING
An imprint of Little Tiger Press
1 The Coda Centre, 189 Munster Road,
London SW6 6AW

This hardback edition first published
in Great Britain in 2015.

Text copyright © Holly Webb, 2015
Illustrations copyright © Artful Doodlers, 2015
Cover illustration copyright © Simon Mendez, 2015
Author photograph copyright © Nigel Bird
*Holly Webb Animal Stories* illustrations copyright © Sophy Williams
*My Naughty Little Puppy* illustration copyright © Kate Pankhurst

ISBN: 978-1-84715-607-5

A CIP catalogue record for this book is available
from the British Library.

Printed and bound in the UK.

2 4 6 8 10 9 7 5 3

# The
# *Storm*
# *Leopards*

## HOLLY WEBB

Stripes

For Lauren and Katelyn

~ HOLLY WEBB

To Hannah - with big thanks

~ JO

# CHAPTER
# ONE

I sabelle watched the group of children move off down the road, jingling their collection tins. The pavement was slippery with frost and icy puddles, and one of the girls nearly skidded over. A couple of the others grabbed her to hold her up and they all giggled.

*If I was still back at home, I'd be out carol singing with my friends, too*, Isabelle thought. She closed the front door and leaned against it with a sigh. Some of the children from her old school went to the old people's home to sing carols at this time of year. Probably her friends would be doing that this week. Isabelle blinked at the Christmas cards hanging on a string along the banisters. Lucy had sent her one, and Ellie – really lovely, glittery cards, with long messages about how much they missed her and how school wasn't the same without her. And her friends had both made her laugh – she could almost hear them talking to her. But it was nothing like being back home with them, not really.

Isabelle had spotted a couple of people from her new class when she'd opened the door – one of the boys had recognized her and waved, which was nice. But she still felt like an outsider. She hadn't been invited to join in. Nobody at this school knew that she loved singing.

"Wasn't that nice?" Isabelle's mum came back out of the kitchen, smiling. The carol singers had been collecting for the children's ward at the local hospital, and Mum had just gone to put her purse away. "I feel so Christmassy now!"

Isabelle nodded. She wanted to feel Christmassy, too. It was just that she felt so sad at the same time.

Her little sister, Tilly, was galloping up and down the hallway singing, "Little Donkey! Little Donkey!" and then neighing loudly. It was her favourite Christmas carol, but Tilly was only four, and she couldn't remember any more of the words.

"It's 'Little Donkey, carry Mary,'" Isabelle tried to tell her, but Tilly wasn't listening.

"There's no point," her mum whispered. "Come and have some hot chocolate. The carol singing was beautiful, but it was cold standing at the door to listen. I wouldn't be surprised if it snowed soon – they did say it might on the weather forecast. That's one of the nice things about being further up north now, isn't it? And I bet the snow stays cleaner here, too. It won't go slushy and brown like it does in the city."

Isabelle didn't say anything. She didn't think that the snow would make up for missing all her friends, and having to start a new school a few weeks before Christmas. Her parents had explained everything to her and Tilly – how they were moving so Mum and Dad could run their own shop instead of working for someone else. How exciting it was. And it meant they'd be living really close to Gran and Grandad. That was a good thing, Isabelle had to admit. But it was on a visit to Gran and Grandad that her mum and dad had seen that the little cake shop they'd always loved was for sale. If only they hadn't walked down that street that day!

Isabelle's mum placed a mug of hot chocolate down in front of her, and then put an arm round her shoulders. "I know you're missing the things you'd have been doing back at the old house, Isabelle. But there's fun things happening here, too. It's the special Christmas event at the zoo tomorrow – with the reindeer, remember?"

Isabelle nodded and smiled at her. The hot chocolate was really good – thick and sweet, and Mum had even put marshmallows on top. She was trying so hard. But Christmas just didn't feel Christmassy here, even with the promise of snow.

Isabelle laughed as the penguin swam past, eyeing the visitors curiously through the glass panel set into the side of the tank.

Tilly danced up and down, squeaking, "Look, look, did you see, Belle? Did you see him? Do you think he likes my hat?" Tilly adored penguins – she was wearing her penguin hat and mittens, and she had been looking forward to seeing them all day, even more than seeing Father Christmas's reindeer.

That was another of the good things about their new home, Isabelle told herself firmly. The zoo was just outside the town, really not far away at all, and there were always special events and fun things to do. Her mum had said that they could come and visit lots.

Tilly now had her nose pressed up against the glass, and she and Mum and Dad were all cooing at the penguins. Isabelle liked them, too, but the smell was getting to her a bit.

"Mum…" She tapped her mum's arm. "Can I go and see whatever's on the other side of the path? That big enclosure with all the trees and rocks in? I won't go wandering off, I promise."

Her mum glanced over at the tall enclosure, which looked as though it had been built around the side of a little hill. "You will be careful, won't you? Stay right there? We won't be more than five minutes; we'll catch you up."

Actually, Isabelle thought, they didn't have a chance of getting Tilly away from the penguins in five minutes, but she didn't say so. "See you in a bit," she told Mum and hurried up the steps from the penguin tank, glad to get away from the fishy stink. Probably at the South Pole penguins didn't smell as bad, she imagined. It was cold enough there to get rid of all the fishiness.

Once she was out on the path, the chilly wind blew the smell away, and she took a deep breath. Maybe Mum was right, and it would snow soon. The sky had that heavy, greyish-yellow look to it.

"Hello … Isabelle?" someone said, just behind her, and Isabelle spun round in surprise. The girl was so wrapped up in a big furry hat and a woolly scarf that it took Isabelle a moment to recognize her – it was one of the girls from her class at school.

"Hi," Isabelle said, a little shyly. Why couldn't she remember this girl's name? Daisy? Lottie? "Have you come to see the reindeer?" she asked.

The girl nodded. "Sort of. My riding school helps out with the Christmas parade that they have this afternoon. You know, with Father Christmas in his sleigh? The riding school lends all the ponies. I'm taking part in it, which is great, but I have to dress up in an elf costume. Promise you won't laugh at me!"

"Oh, I won't." Isabelle shook her head. "You're so lucky, going to a riding school. I've only been a couple of times on holiday – there wasn't a stables anywhere near our old house."

"You should come to Hill Farm," the other girl told her. "It's brilliant. You could come with me the first time, so you weren't all on your own."

"Daisy! Come on!" A man was waving at them, and Daisy grinned at Isabelle. "Got to go, I told my dad I'd only be a minute. I just wanted to say hello. See you later! Remember – promise no laughing at my stupid costume!"

"OK!" Isabelle smiled and watched as Daisy dashed away. A riding stables, close by! And Daisy had said Isabelle could go with her – she'd really sounded like she meant it, too. Isabelle walked over to the enclosure, still with a smile on her face, feeling better than she had in days.

She was a lot happier than most of the people standing at the barrier around the wire fence, she realized, after a minute or so of peering through at the trees beyond. One family was walking off looking really disappointed, and everyone else seemed to be drifting away, too. Perhaps whatever lived here didn't want to be seen? The wire fence went all the way round the huge enclosure, which was planted with trees and bushes, and even had a little stream running down among the dark rocks. The animals that lived here would be able to hide quite easily if they wanted to.

"Maybe it's too cold to come out," Isabelle murmured to herself. She didn't mind. She could go back to the penguins, and tell Mum and Dad about the riding school. Dad had said it would be really good to find some fun new activities once they were properly settled.

But just as she was turning away, she caught a flash of movement among the bushes. Curious, Isabelle leaned forward, gazing through the wire. Whatever it was had pale grey fur, and it looked quite big. Isabelle held her breath and watched as the creature stepped out – and stared at her with glowing green-gold eyes.

"A leopard..." Isabelle breathed. But it wasn't, not quite. She had seen pictures of leopards, and they were long and lean and golden, with short, silky-looking fur. This cat had a small, neat head, but the rest of her was almost stocky, with huge silvery paws and a fluffy white chest. She was dappled with black spots, and her tail was long and fat. It waved behind her like a thick furry scarf.

The big cat gazed at Isabelle with great, round eyes, like green glass marbles. Then she turned and loped proudly away between the rocks, leaving Isabelle staring after her, open-mouthed.

"That wasn't just a leopard," Isabelle whispered. She was still peering hopefully through the wire, but the silver-grey cat had disappeared. Isabelle shivered as the cold wind cut through her coat. "I wonder what you are?" she said to herself, stuffing her hands into her pockets and hurrying over to the display board at the front of the enclosure. "Oh! A *snow* leopard!" *I didn't even know you could get snow leopards...* She frowned. Didn't leopards live in jungles – or forests, at least? The spots were for camouflage amongst the leaves, she'd thought. She giggled, thinking of a snow leopard trying to camouflage itself in the snow – it would be like a lot of floating spots...

*Actually, I suppose snow isn't white all the time*, Isabelle decided, looking thoughtfully at the rocky enclosure. *Maybe the spots do help them blend in, if they live in rocky sorts of places like this.* She scanned the display eagerly, looking at the photos of the leopards' habitat, and the map showing where they lived in the wild. China, Russia, Nepal, India. "All across the Himalayas... Mountain cats." Isabelle glanced up at the rocks again, and caught her breath – was that a silvery face gazing down at her between the branches, or had she just imagined it?

The wind shifted the trees a little, and there was nothing there. But even though she couldn't see the snow leopard, Isabelle was sure that she was still listening and watching.

"I can see why you need all that fur," she said. "It looks so cosy, just right for snowy mountains." Then she went back to reading. The poster said that snow leopards used their furry tails as scarves to wrap around their noses. Isabelle hitched her own scarf higher up. "Good plan," she whispered through the fence.

"What are you looking at?" Mum said behind her, and Isabelle jumped.

"Oh! I was reading this – all about snow leopards. This one's called Dara."

"It's cute!" Tilly said, pointing at the photos. "Where is it?" And she tried to lean over the barrier and get closer to the wire. "I can't see it. I want to see the big cat!"

"She could be asleep, Tilly." Mum crouched down beside her to explain. "There are caves and dens for the leopard to sleep in. I read about her on the zoo's website – it said that snow leopards are really shy. Sometimes they don't want to be seen. We're really lucky to have one here in the zoo to look at – in the wild, people hardly ever see them."

"But I want her to come out and see me!" Tilly said crossly. "It's not fair!"

"Only five thousand left in the wild," Isabelle's dad murmured, looking at the information board. "Wow, they definitely are endangered. But it says they've been breeding them here for quite a while."

Isabelle nodded. "Dara was born here at the zoo, it says. And she had cubs, but now they're older they've gone to other zoos – because snow leopards like to be on their own in their territory. And they want to get zoos all over the world to breed them, because they're so rare."

"They're shy, Tilly. You'd never see

one if you went to their mountains, either," Dad said, putting an arm round Tilly, who was still looking sulky. "Even here in the zoo they don't always want to show themselves. Now, we'd better go if we want to get a good spot to watch this parade. We can come again – we'll just have to make sure we look for Dara every time we visit. I'm sure we'll see her sooner or later, won't we, Belle?"

*But I did see her...* Isabelle almost said aloud. Then she simply smiled and nodded, and followed her family.

"Goodbye," she whispered, as they headed away from the enclosure. The snow leopard would be her secret. As she walked slowly down the path, she was sure that a pale-furred cat was watching her go, hidden deep among the rocks.

# CHAPTER TWO

"Isabelle, there's an elf waving at you over there…" Dad nudged her. "Look, on that white pony." He pointed over the shoulder of the lady next to him, and Isabelle leaned over the fence to see. There was a big crowd gathered to watch the parade, but they'd managed to find a good place. Even Tilly could see, peering through the barrier.

"They're called grey, Dad," Isabelle said, smiling. The pony was gorgeous, almost snow-white, with a long forelock that dropped over his eyes. He had a Christmassy red and green blanket under his saddle, and tassels hanging off his reins. Daisy had on stripy red-and-white tights and a green tunic. She even had a little pointy elf hat. Isabelle sucked her cheeks in hard – she'd promised she wouldn't laugh.

"Is she a friend from school?" Dad asked, glancing at Isabelle hopefully. "She's a very good rider. They all look amazing, actually. Those ponies must be very well trained to stay so calm with all these children cheering at them."

"She's not quite a friend yet," Isabelle said. "But she might be. I think, anyway. She said maybe I could go riding with her," she added, grinning at Daisy. She was making faces at her cute elf outfit and mouthing something that looked like, *Don't you dare laugh!*

"What about one of these necklaces?" Isabelle's mum suggested. "With the owls on – so sweet!"

"Maybe," Isabelle said. Mum had

given both her and Tilly a bit of money to spend in the gift shop – not loads, because it was just before Christmas, but enough for a small souvenir. Tilly was with Dad, trying to decide between sweets and a furry penguin, but Isabelle just couldn't find anything she really liked.

She peered into a basket on one of the shelves – it looked like there were little fabric toys in it. Isabelle picked one out, wondering if Tilly would like it, and then smiled delightedly – a little felt cat.

"That's pretty," her mum commented. "It's a Christmas decoration – look." She pointed out the loop of thread on the cat's back. "You could put it on the tree, or hang it up in your room."

Isabelle turned the little cat over, surprised by the roughness of the felt under her fingers. She looked at the big label attached to the cat's back, wondering whether the felt was made of something strange. It didn't feel like the felt they used to make things at school. The label showed a photo of a family, wearing strange wrap-around coats and beaming at the camera. The girl in the photo was about the same age as she was. She had two tall older brothers, and she looked tiny standing in between them.

"Handmade in Mongolia," Isabelle read. "Mum, these are sold by a snow leopard charity – it says so, look!" She smiled, stroking the dark spots on the pale blue felt. "I thought it was a cat, but it's a snow leopard. Please can I buy this?" She checked the price. "I've got enough."

She followed her mum to the till, still reading the label. The tree ornaments were made by families in Mongolia, it explained. People who lived in the snow leopards' habitat. The charity sold the decorations for them, which meant that they were sold in a larger number of shops. That way the families earned more, and in return they agreed not to hunt the snow leopards. Instead they helped to care for them as a protected species.

Isabelle handed over her money, and

then went back to reading the label. At the bottom there was a website address. She would look it up as soon as she got home, she decided. *What must it be like, to live among the snow leopards?* she wondered.

Isabelle stood the little felt snow leopard on the desk in her bedroom. She'd borrowed Mum's laptop to look up the snow leopard charity online. She still couldn't believe that she hadn't even known snow leopards existed – Isabelle loved animals and she knew loads about wildlife, or she'd thought she did. Well, she was going to make up for it now.

Isabelle typed in the address from the label and gave a delighted gasp at the beautiful photo that came up on the screen

— a snow leopard sitting on a hillside, staring out across a valley at a line of snow-topped mountains. His fur was yellowish cream, dappled with soft ash-grey spots and rings, and his tail curled out behind him, looking almost as long as he was.

The charity's website had lots of photos and a whole area for snow leopard information, too. Isabelle skipped from page to page, cooing at the gorgeous pictures. The cubs were even cuter than the adult snow leopards. They looked more like normal leopards than the adults did, but Isabelle wasn't quite sure why. Maybe because all leopard cubs had massive paws and much fluffier fur than grown-up leopards.

"Aww," Isabelle whispered. "They're born with blue eyes, like Tilly was." Isabelle had been surprised when her little sister was born – she and Mum and Dad all had dark hair and eyes, but Tilly's eyes were a soft blue. They'd changed to brown now, and Mum had told her that most white babies had blue eyes at first.

It looked like it was the same for snow leopards – almost all the adults had eyes that were grey, or greenish like the snow leopard at the zoo.

She clicked on Frequently Asked Questions, wondering if it said how many snow leopards there were in the world. The zoo display board had said there were only about five thousand wild snow leopards. It didn't sound like very many at all.

There – between four thousand and six and a half thousand, it said. And they were at risk from all sorts of things. Isabelle read the article with a tightness in her throat. Those beautiful cats – so many people seemed to want to hurt them, or just didn't care if they got hurt. How could people hunt snow leopards for their fur, especially when there were so few of them left? Isabelle shivered. She thought the creamy spotted fur was gorgeous, but she couldn't imagine wanting to wear it.

"Isabelle, it's bedtime." Mum put her head round the bedroom door. "Are you all right?" She came in and eyed Isabelle worriedly. "Belle, what's wrong? You look so sad."

"I was reading about snow leopards." Isabelle sniffed. "It just seems like everybody wants to hunt them. People even want to use their bones in medicines – did you know that?"

"Oh, Isabelle." Her mum leaned down to give her a hug. "I suppose at least we're helping a bit by buying the Christmas decoration. We can hang it on the tree, when we put it up tomorrow."

"But there are so few of them left…" Isabelle looked at the picture on her screen – a snow leopard dozing with its chin on a boulder. *How did anyone get that close to take the picture?* she wondered. The snow leopard looked like any cat, slumped and snoozing in the sunshine. It had a gorgeous apricot-pink nose, and a spray of delicate black spots across the creamy fur on its chin. Isabelle wished she could sit next to it and stroke that soft-looking muzzle.

She picked up the little felt snow leopard and rubbed one finger across its head. Somehow, just buying a Christmas decoration didn't seem like enough, she thought, as she hugged her mum goodnight and began to get ready for bed. Once she had her pyjamas on, Isabelle tucked the little leopard beneath her pillow. Then she curled up under her duvet, with her fingers round the cat's stubby tail, and sighed. How was she ever going to get to sleep when there were gorgeous spotted cats dancing around inside her head?

# CHAPTER
# THREE

Isabelle rolled over and pressed her cheek into the warmth of her pillow. It was still really dark – and it was a Sunday; she didn't need to get up yet... But there was a noise. She blinked sleepily, trying to work out what it was.

Someone was crying.

Isabelle sat up, listening. Was it Tilly having a bad dream? Isabelle hesitated for a moment. Mum and Dad obviously hadn't heard her. Isabelle sighed. Her bed was so warm – and it was very, very cold in her bedroom. Much colder than it had been the night before, actually. Perhaps Mum had been right, and it had snowed?

Another burst of sobbing made Isabelle wriggle out of bed, shivering as she pulled off the duvet. Poor Tilly! She sounded so upset. She sounded like she was nearby, too, Isabelle realized, shaking her head and yawning. Tilly must have got out of bed. She definitely wasn't in her own bedroom across the landing any more – Isabelle could tell that the snuffling, heaving breaths were really close. Perhaps Tilly had come into her room. She did sometimes climb into bed with Isabelle if she wanted a cuddle.

Isabelle peered around her bedroom, squinting at the shadowy shapes of the furniture. It looked – different. But that was the dark. It made everything look strange. Isabelle had once woken up in the night and spent a whole ten minutes being absolutely terrified of her own wardrobe.

Someone cried again – a heartbreaking little catch of breath.

"Where are you, Tilly?" Isabelle

whispered. "Are you on the end of my bed? I can't see you. Did you have a bad dream?"

There was silence – no more crying. But Isabelle was sure that Tilly was there, and had heard her. It was a listening sort of silence. As though Tilly was holding her breath.

"I'm not cross. What's wrong?" Isabelle blinked again. She was getting used to the darkness now and she could almost see. There was a lump at the end of the bed – definitely someone lying there. "Come and have a cuddle, Tilly." Isabelle climbed back into bed, pulling the duvet up around her shoulders. She shivered again – it was so cold – and huddled closer into the duvet, wishing it was thicker. It felt odd.

Isabelle was just realizing that the duvet wasn't her duvet, when the small lump at the end of the bed unrolled itself and sat up – and she saw that her sister wasn't her sister, either.

It was another girl – a complete stranger.

Isabelle swallowed slowly. Her eyes were properly accustomed to the early morning dimness now, and she could see quite well. It wasn't that there was a stranger sitting on the end of her bed – *she* was the stranger.

It wasn't her bed, or her bedroom, or her house. In fact, the bed probably belonged to the confused, tear-stained girl who was staring at her.

Isabelle opened her mouth to explain – to say sorry, that she'd made a mistake. And then she shut it again. She couldn't explain, not at all. For a moment she wondered if she'd gone sleepwalking. She had done it, once before. Her mum had told her all about it afterwards, how she'd come downstairs, asleep but with her eyes open, and Mum had had to try and persuade her back to bed. But that had been such a long time ago – and even if she'd managed to sleepwalk out of her own house and into someone else's, this room didn't look like any room she'd ever seen before.

The girl reached down to the side of the bed, and Isabelle flinched back, wondering what she was doing. But when she sat up again, she had a little light in her hands – a torch. She was shading it with her fingers, as though she didn't want it to be too bright.

Isabelle blinked in the glow and looked around slowly, still trying to work out what sort of place she'd turned up in.

It was *round*. There was a stove in the middle, with a tall metal chimney – a bit like the black iron wood-burning stove at Gran and Grandad's house, but this one was shiny metal, the front of it cut into patterns, like stars. The chimney led up out of a hole in the ceiling. That was strangely old-fashioned – but then there was a fridge, up against the wall, and a television on a wooden chest. And there were more beds, with people still sleeping in them, ranged around the edges of the room.

The girl rubbed a hand across her eyes – to wipe away the tears, Isabelle thought, or perhaps to wipe away this strange dream-girl who was sitting in front of her.

A dream! That was it! Isabelle felt the tight fear in her chest ease a little. It was a dream, of course it was. She was dreaming all this and she would wake up soon. She took a deep, slightly shaky breath and smiled at the other girl.

"Hello." Then she nibbled her bottom lip nervously, wondering if the girl would understand her. She was wearing pyjamas that weren't all that different from Isabelle's own, with a sparkly dog on the front of them, but she didn't look quite like anyone Isabelle had ever met. She did remind Isabelle a bit of Lucy, who was half Chinese, but this girl's skin was more tanned than Lucy's. And she lived in this strange round room.

"Hello," the other girl said back, shyly. She looked confused – as though she'd woken up, but her dream hadn't gone away.

Isabelle's smile widened in relief – so she did talk English. Or actually, Isabelle decided, since this was a dream, she must be talking whatever the other girl's language was. Or something. At any rate, they seemed to understand each other.

"Sarangerel?" The girl looked at Isabelle hopefully, and Isabelle's smile slipped. She didn't understand, then! Perhaps the girl had just repeated hello to be polite. What did "Sarangerel" mean?

"You *are* Sarangerel? I've never seen you for real before, only spoken to you… But you must be her," said the girl.

Isabelle hesitated, torn between relief that the girl seemed to speak the same language she did after all, and a reluctance to say that yes, she was Sarangerel. The girl seemed to want her to be Sarangerel so much. She was leaning forward now, reaching out her hand to Isabelle across the pile of patterned quilts and blankets. Her narrow dark eyes had widened hopefully, and she was smiling, even though there were still tear-tracks down her cheeks.

"I'm so glad you've come. I need someone to talk to, and even though I used to talk to you all the time, it's so much easier now you're real."

"Yes..." Isabelle agreed. She could understand that. But who was this Sarangerel?

"I haven't talked to you for years," the girl murmured. "I don't know how long. I suppose you're here because everything's going wrong. You knew I needed you..."

Isabelle blinked, suddenly wondering if Sarangerel was the girl's imaginary friend. Tilly had one – every so often Isabelle heard her talking to someone called Herbie. Tilly said he lived in America, and he came to visit, and he only ever ate popcorn (which was Tilly's favourite food). But thinking about it, Tilly did tend to talk to Herbie when she was upset. He cheered her up.

*This is the strangest dream I've ever had,* Isabelle thought. There was so much in it. Things Isabelle didn't think she'd be able to imagine, like this odd room. The walls weren't papered, the way she'd thought at first. The red flower pattern was fabric, hanging up, and here and there she could see a wooden trellis, like the trellis her mum had in the garden for growing clematis.

But it was as if the walls were made out of it – with fabric on the outside, too.

*A tent*, she thought to herself. *A really big, round tent. Like a tipi.* And then it came back to her – of course, dreams were like that. You put things in them that you'd been thinking about the day before. It wasn't just a tent, or a tipi, it was a *ger*. The same sort of tent that the Mongolian nomads used, the people who lived in snow leopard country. The people who'd made her little felt snow leopard. She had been thinking about snow leopards, and the people who lived so close to them, just before she went to sleep. It made sense that she'd dream about them. It was just a dream. Somehow, working that out made her feel much better. "Yes, I'm Sarangerel," she told the other girl.

"Maybe you've come now because of the full moon," the girl said thoughtfully. "I was looking up at it last night and wishing so hard. It is your name, after all. Sarangerel means moonlight. I called you that when I was little because it was the prettiest name I could think of."

Isabelle nodded. It would help if the girl would say what her own name was, but Isabelle couldn't really ask – not if she was supposed to be her imaginary friend. It might spoil the dream, and she didn't really want to wake up yet. Now that she wasn't frightened any more, this was the most interesting dream she'd ever had.

"Why were you wishing?" she whispered, glancing around at the other sleeping people.

The girl's face seemed to crumple, and she hung her head. "I don't know what to do," she whispered back.

"Tell me what's wrong," Isabelle said, settling cautiously back against the trellis wall, with the quilts pulled up around her chin.

"Three of our goats are dead," the girl explained, her voice shaking a little.

"Oh… Did you really love them?" Isabelle asked sympathetically. There had been goats at the zoo, in the petting area. The little ones were very cute. "Did they have names?"

The girl looked up at her in surprise. "No, of course not. We don't name our goats. We don't even name the horses. Why would we? The dogs have names, that's all. And I didn't love those goats more than any of the others. It's just that we can't afford to lose them."

Isabelle nodded slowly and decided she'd better not say too much. Everything was so different here, it would be easy to make another silly mistake.

"You can't afford to lose them…" she prompted the girl.

"No, because we need to sell the meat

and use their wool for the toymaking. We haven't got so much money that we can just lose three goats and it doesn't matter!" She gave a miserable little snort.

"What happened to them?" Isabelle asked, hoping that this wasn't another silly question.

"My pa thinks it was wolves, but my uncle Erdene, who herds with us, he thinks it was a snow leopard, from the way the goats looked."

Isabelle gasped, and the girl glanced up at her and nodded. "They don't know for sure. The dogs barked, and Pa ran out with his gun and scared whatever it was away." She sniffed, and Isabelle saw tears trickle down her cheeks.

"I don't understand..." Isabelle whispered. "I know it's terrible that something killed the goats – but I don't see why you're so upset." The way the girl was crying reminded Isabelle of how she'd been the day they moved house. Or worse, the day before that, when she'd said goodbye to Lucy and Ellie. It wasn't the way someone cried over a goat that was definitely just a goat and not a pet. "You're crying like you've lost something you really love," she said at last, trying to put it into words.

The girl brushed the tears off her cheeks and nodded. "Yes. I haven't yet, but I think I'm going to." She looked searchingly at Isabelle, and then stretched out her hand. "I'll have to show you. Then you'll understand. You're Sarangerel, of course you'll understand. Come on."

# CHAPTER
# FOUR

The girl gently pulled Isabelle by the hand over to a chest at the foot of the bed. There was a rumpled pile of thick cloth lying on it and a pair of boots lined up there, too. The girl looked Isabelle up and down thoughtfully. "You're a bit smaller than me," she murmured, picking up the bundle and shaking it out. She handed Isabelle the torch to hold and quickly slipped her arms into the sleeves. It was a coat, Isabelle realized. Or maybe a dressing gown? It wrapped over at the front and buttoned up. The girl tied a sash around her middle and then lifted the lid on the wooden chest, making the painted flowers across the top dance in the torchlight. She pulled out another bundle, and held it out to Isabelle.

"This *deel* should fit you. It's nice and

warm. And you can try on the boots I've just grown out of, look." She put them down in front of Isabelle's feet. "Hurry, though. We don't want my ma to wake up."

Isabelle did as she was told, pushing her feet into the leather boots. She was glad she'd put on her fluffy socks at bedtime. The girl held up the *deel* and showed Isabelle how to put it on, guiding her arms into the sleeves and giggling a little as Isabelle tried to understand how the strange bobbles fitted into their holes. In the end, the girl did them up for her and wrapped the sash around her waist, too. "Good, it fits," she murmured.

Isabelle held out her hands, showing the girl the way the sleeves flapped over them. "Can you help me turn them up?" she whispered.

"No, don't be silly, you want them like that, to keep your hands warm."

"Oh." Isabelle nodded. Extra-long sleeves instead of gloves. She shivered a little, even though the coat was thick and padded. She thought it was probably made of wool, or at least the lining was.

"Come on." The girl led Isabelle over to the door of the tent – a proper wooden front door, Isabelle noticed, frowning to herself. This was nothing like the tent Mum and Dad had for camping holidays. But then, her family only ever spent weekends in theirs. This was more like a cross between a tent and a house.

The girl stepped carefully over the doorframe and out into the early morning mist. Isabelle almost stumbled as she followed her outside.

"Mind the threshold," the girl murmured, catching her arm. "Bad luck, remember."

Isabelle hardly heard her. The view was like nothing she had ever seen. They were surrounded by snow-covered mountains, rising up out of the mist. Great snowy crags ringed the grassy terrace, pink and grey and shadowed in the early light of the morning. The dark rocks looming

above them were seamed with snow, but
around the white tents, there were only
small patches dotted about.

"Why isn't it all snow-covered here?" Isabelle whispered to the girl.

"Because the mountain protects us from the wind. That's why we have our winter camp up here. Come on." She pulled Isabelle after her, and they began to head away from the flattish grass where the four *gers* were pitched. At least, it looked flat compared to the jagged mountains all around, but Isabelle guessed that the *gers* must be in exactly the same places every year. Someone must have cleared the rocks and boulders away from those circular patches to fit the tents in. There was plenty of long, scrubby sort of grass, but it was growing in and around the rocks, and as the girl began to lead her up and away from the *gers*, the rocks grew thicker, and the grass petered out entirely.

The girl stopped to pat a dog that loomed up at them out of the shadows, and Isabelle looked at him worriedly. But all he did was sniff at them, and then he trotted away, obviously deciding they weren't a threat.

"He's guarding the sheep," the girl whispered. "The snow leopard or wolf, whatever it was, it got past the dogs."

"Where are we going?" Isabelle asked, tucking her hands up inside the long sleeves and huddling into the warm, padded coat. It was painfully cold, even though there was a little pale sunlight shining on the snow.

"Further up the mountain, so I can show you. But you'd better hold my hand – it's steep here."

Isabelle nodded gratefully. The girl

was a very good climber, even without any special sort of equipment, no ropes or gripping gloves, or anything like that. She was just wearing leather boots, and she had quite a long coat on – the *deel* – but she could scramble over rocks much better than Isabelle. She giggled as she hauled Isabelle up after her. At one point, she even came round behind Isabelle to push her up a scree slope, a whole hillside of wobbly stones that seemed to want to slip out from under Isabelle's boots at every step.

"I'm not very good – at climbing things," Isabelle panted. "Sorry. It's so slidey."

"Lean forward more. And use your hands. We're not far now, don't worry. And look, we'll stop here for a moment."

They seemed to be on a flatter path now, and Isabelle felt the girl clutch her hand tightly. Then she bowed her head a little towards a tapering pile of rocks, taller than they were, which stood at the side of the faintly worn path. At first Isabelle had thought that it was just a heap of boulders that had fallen down, but now she had caught her breath and could look at it properly, she saw that it had been built.

"Oh, a cairn," she said, smiling as she recognized what it was. Gran and Grandad had taken them on a walk in the hills back in the summer – not nearly as hard a walk as this one. There had been a very nice teashop at the end of it, which Isabelle suspected there wouldn't be here – and there had been a cairn. Grandad had told them that when people walked past they would add a stone to the pile, so it grew bigger every year.

"It's an *obo*," the girl corrected her. "To honour the mountain."

"But you add a rock to it, when you go past?"

"Yes. Or another offering. Bottles, look, and streamers."

The streamers were made out of strips of plastic, and they fluttered in the gusty wind. "It's pretty." Isabelle smiled. "Can we put stones on it?"

"Of course. And perhaps the spirits will help us find what we're looking for." The girl nodded thoughtfully and picked up a stone.

Isabelle chose a greyish piece of rock, patterned with stripes, that happened to be close to her foot – perhaps a really pretty rock made a better offering?

"We walk round it, three times," the girl said, leading her around the *obo*. "And now we put our stones on."

Isabelle placed her striped stone gently on the side of the tall pile and held her breath for a second, hoping that it wouldn't all fall down.

"Who is it for?" she asked quietly, and then wished she hadn't when the girl gave her a strange, doubting look.

"I thought you'd know about that kind of thing," she murmured. "Although I suppose you're not really a spirit, because I made you up... I don't know what you are."

*Nor do I*, Isabelle thought worriedly.

How could she be dreaming all these things if she didn't know about them when she was awake? It had seemed quite reasonable before, but she most certainly hadn't read about *obos* when she was looking up snow leopards. *But it can't be anything else than a dream*, she told herself firmly. *It's just a strange one, that's all.*

The girl looked around uncertainly, as though she wasn't sure how to explain. "The *obo*... It's for the mountain. And the sky. Everything – it's all important."

She frowned, obviously trying to work out how to explain. "It's like the flag," she added suddenly. "Mongolia's flag has all colours to mean different things. Blue is the sky, of course, and yellow is the sun. Green is the grass that feeds our animals and red is fire. White is the sacred colour, the colour of the spirits. That's why white is the most special colour for foods, like milk. I'll give you milk and curds when we get back. That's what we always give to guests."

Isabelle nodded. It did make sense. Her mum kept saying since they'd moved how lovely it was to see the sky and the grass on the hills. She said it made her feel like she could breathe. Dad always rolled his eyes and said he was a city boy, but Isabelle knew he liked it, too.

Isabelle patted her rock gently. She felt at home here, just a little, now that she'd seen the *obo*. It was something that felt familiar. The *ger* was so strange, even if it was warm and cosy like her own house, and it did have a fridge and a TV. Isabelle was sure she had seen a motorbike, too, parked under a little shelter with a plastic roof. It was the odd way that all these familiar things were put together that made them seem frighteningly different.

"There's one last climb," the girl explained, leading Isabelle along the rocky path.

Isabelle tried not to sigh. Her legs ached already.

"It's worth it, I promise. You'll see why it's so important." The girl gave a little gulp, and Isabelle saw that her eyes had filled with tears again. The fun of the climb together had cheered her up, Isabelle realized. But now the girl had remembered what it was that had made her lie there crying in the dark.

Isabelle did her best to climb after the girl, refusing to let herself complain or show that she was tired, even though her hands hurt from trying to grab at the frozen rocks. There was more snow here as they climbed around the side of the mountain, out of its shelter.

"Wait," the girl said at last. "We can't get too close. Here is good. Look, just sit and watch. Up there." She glanced worriedly at Isabelle's pinched face and wrapped an arm round her, snuggling her close to warm her up. "Just watch. It's not long after dawn, and they often come then. Dawn and dusk are the best times."

*Who does?* Isabelle wondered, leaning against the girl's shoulder. The cold was making her feel dazed and dreamy. "Who comes?" she whispered.

"Wait and see. Soon…"

Isabelle yawned and felt her eyes closing. Perhaps when she woke up, she would be in her own bed again? But then the girl shook her gently. "Sarangerel, look. Up above us."

Isabelle straightened up and tried to

look where the girl was pointing, at a rocky crag above the thin little patch of path they sat on. It seemed like any other ledge – she couldn't see what was so special about it. Although that spot of darkness at the end of the ledge could be a cave, perhaps.

And then out of the cave, slowly, cautiously, padded a ghost-like creature, her thick tail swinging gracefully behind her.

"A snow leopard!" Isabelle breathed, suddenly awake. She was actually seeing one, in the wild! The beautiful cat was only metres away.

"Watch!" The girl nudged her excitedly, and Isabelle could hear in her voice that she was smiling.

After the great grey cat tumbled two

smaller cubs, yellowish-grey and spotted like their mother. They didn't seem to be as cautious as she was, and they bounced happily along the ledge, nipping and scuffling, until she turned back to glare at them and cuff the larger cub with one huge paw. It hissed a little, and then dived underneath its mother to jump in front of the smaller cub.

"They're so beautiful," Isabelle murmured. "The littlest cub has blue eyes, look!"

The girl nodded. "I named her Sky – her eyes are just that deep summer blue."

"What about the others?" Isabelle asked, holding back a laugh as Sky squared up to the larger cub with a gruff growl. The deep noise sounded strange coming from something so small. Sky was perhaps the size of a little dog, Isabelle thought, trying to measure in her head. Spaniel-sized. And the other cub was a bit bigger.

"Her brother – I think he's her brother, anyway – he's called Shadow. And the mother is Grace, because of the way she moves. I've been coming here to see them for months. Since the cubs were tiny."

"I never thought they'd be so close to your home," Isabelle said, watching the mother snow leopard sink down on the rocky ledge, while the cubs clambered around and over her, jumping and wrestling. The smaller cub peered over the ridge at the girls, and Isabelle saw her blue eyes shining. Could she see them looking at her?

"They're well hidden, though," the girl said. "I think they probably know we're here – they must be able to smell us – but they're used to seeing me now."

"How did you find them? Or does everyone know where they are?"

"Oh no." The girl looked shocked. "And you mustn't tell." Then she let out a breath of a laugh. "Of course, I forgot. No one can hear you except for me. At least, no one ever could before."

Isabelle nodded. "They're your secret?"

"Mmm-hmm. I found them back in the summer. I was looking for one of our goats that had strayed. We were camped a lot further down the mountain then, and it was a long way up here. It was fun being out on my own. I love our *ger*, but there's so many people around, and my brothers are always telling me what to do because they're bigger than I am."

Isabelle's eyes widened. Two big brothers – just like the picture on her snow leopard's label. Could this be the same girl? Isabelle tried to remember the tiny photo she'd seen. She thought it was... And Isabelle could understand that she'd want some time on her own. A little sister was bossy enough – she couldn't imagine two big brothers telling her what to do all the time.

"I was having an adventure by myself. So, well, when I couldn't find the goat I didn't go straight home, I went on exploring. I got tired and I sat down to rest for a bit – I almost fell asleep, and then I heard a scraping noise and pebbles bouncing. When I looked up, I saw the snow leopard going into her den! I stayed and watched her – I'd never seen a snow leopard before, and she was so beautiful, so clever, the way she leaped up the rocks. And then I saw her cubs! They were tiny then, little fluffy things. After that I came to watch them whenever I could. I was lucky it wasn't too far from any of our pastures, even when we moved." She sighed. "I love them – can you tell? But my family calls them the ghosts of the mountain. Beautiful and deadly. They say that the mother killed the goats."

"Do you think she did?"

The girl sighed. "Maybe. She's got two cubs to feed, so she can't go as far as she would on her own looking for food. I've seen her leave them and go off to hunt, and she brought back a wild sheep, an *argali*.

They aren't so very different from our sheep and goats – it's just that they've got curly horns. How should she know the difference?" She swallowed miserably. "Some of the men in our camp want to kill her before she does it again." The girl put her hands over her face, and Isabelle had to lean close to hear her. "They'll kill Grace, and leave her cubs to die."

# CHAPTER FIVE

"We should go back," the girl whispered at last. She was leaning against Isabelle's shoulder. Even though Isabelle hardly knew her, she'd put her arms round the girl, trying to make her feel better. "Everyone else will be up, now that it's properly light."

Isabelle nodded reluctantly. She didn't want to stop watching the snow leopards playing on the ridge above them. But she could tell that sitting still for any longer wouldn't be a good idea. As it was she could hardly feel her feet, even in the thick leather boots. She grimaced to herself, wondering whether it would be harder to go down the mountain than up. She got to her feet, stiff with cold, and followed the girl as she began to climb carefully down the rocky hillside. The snow leopards caught the sound of their movement at once, and as the girls peered up at the ridge, they saw the mother herding her cubs quickly back to the entrance of the cave.

They picked their way back down, skidding and sliding in places, to the scree slope where the girl had dragged Isabelle on their way up. Isabelle peered down it worriedly and the girl smiled at her. "I'll steady you. We won't fall, I promise."

*It's a dream*, Isabelle told herself, nodding. *I can't fall off a mountain in a dream. Or if I do, it'll just mean I wake up.* But it didn't make her feel much better. The slope was so steep.

She followed the girl gingerly down the slope, hating the feel of the stones shaking under her feet, bouncing away in great frightening leaps. But finally they came to the path, and stood leaning on each other, laughing a little.

Then the girl squinted up at the sky anxiously. The sun was well up now. "We need to hurry and get home. Come on."

They ran along the flat part of the path, and the girl hauled Isabelle down the scrambling climb and across the rock-strewn terrace to the white *gers*, and the pens and stone-built shelters behind them.

"What are those for?" Isabelle asked, looking at the shelters curiously. It seemed odd to live in tents, but have little stone houses behind.

"They're stalls for the horses and the camels," the girl explained.

Isabelle tried not to gape at her. Camels – really?

"Don't they get cold?" Isabelle asked her. "The camels? Aren't they used to it being really hot and sunny?" She thought of camels as desert creatures – but then she remembered the map at the zoo. The mountains weren't that far from the Gobi Desert. She followed the girl round to the front of the stone pens, carefully built away from the wind. A long face stared down at them, fluffy and almost like a teddy bear. The camel had a soft muzzle and big nostrils like a horse, and dark, sly-looking eyes.

"See how much winter wool he has," the girl explained, stroking the camel's nose, while he eyed Isabelle suspiciously. "That keeps him warm, and then he sheds it in the summer when it's really hot. So hot! That's when we grow barley, and vegetables and things. Just a little, in the fields down the mountain, close to the river. It's only for a couple of months, though, so we have to make the best of it. And we use the camels then, for bringing down the summer grass." She giggled. "They look so funny – they carry the grass on their backs in great piles, so they're like big green fuzzy things with legs. Then we dry the grass for the winter, for when we can't take the herd out to graze, you see. They carry the *ger*, too, when we move. Some families have a truck, but my pa thinks it's too expensive, with the petrol as well."

"How can they carry the *ger*?" Isabelle looked doubtfully from the girl to the camel, and the camel stared back at her down his nose, as though he didn't like her much.

"Not the way it is now! It all comes to pieces." The girl snorted with laughter, and Isabelle gave a little sigh. It was all very well to try not to ask questions, but she couldn't help it. The girl must be wondering why she kept asking about everything. Wouldn't an imaginary friend know all these things? Isabelle frowned to herself. Maybe not. Tilly was always explaining stuff to Herbie and bossing him around. She liked being cleverer than he was. Isabelle had a feeling that the girl was just desperate for someone to talk to.

"The horses are here," the girl explained, pulling Isabelle along to the other end of the shelter. There was an eager whinnying sound from inside, and three beautiful horses looked out at them – a dark iron-grey, a chestnut with a white blaze down his nose, and a bay with a shaggy black mane.

"Oh, they're gorgeous," Isabelle whispered, holding out her hand to the dark grey. He sniffed at her fingers and eyed her sideways, clearly not quite sure about her. But then he ducked his head down and let her pet his nose, and he seemed to enjoy the attention.

"You're so lucky," Isabelle said, and the girl smiled at her, but rather sadly.

"Odval! There you are!" A woman about the same age as Isabelle's mum came out of the *ger*, dressed in a dark red *deel*. "Where were you? I was worried!"

Odval! So that was what the girl was called. Then Isabelle gave a little gasp. She looked anxiously at Odval's mother, waiting for her to ask who she was, and how she'd suddenly appeared from nowhere. And why Isabelle was wearing her daughter's old clothes. But Odval's mother didn't even notice her. She just patted Odval's shoulders, looking at her as though she was checking her daughter was all in one piece.

"I only went to the outhouse," the girl – Odval – said innocently, pointing across the terrace to a little white tent. "And then I was just checking if the horses and camels were all right." Isabelle tried not to giggle. Odval was making such a good little girl face. "Shall I turn them out?"

Her mother looked as though she wasn't quite sure whether to believe her, but she shook her head. "No. You'd better hurry inside to help me. Everyone will be here in a minute – they're coming to decide what to do about the snow leopard."

Odval glanced worriedly at Isabelle, and her mother followed her eyes, obviously not sure what she was looking at.

"She can't see me," Isabelle whispered, as Odval's mother turned to go back into the *ger*.

Odval shook her head. "No. It's all right. Only I can."

"The camels and the horses could, too."

Odval frowned. "Yes, I suppose you're right. Maybe animals can see spirits, and people can't? Unless the spirits want them to?"

Isabelle shivered. She wasn't sure she wanted to be called a spirit. "Who's coming to the ger now?"

"Everyone, I think. All the men who'd go hunting the snow leopard, anyway."

"The women don't want to hunt her?" Isabelle asked thoughtfully.

Odval shook her head, and Isabelle could see that she was clenching her fists inside her long sleeves. "No, I'm sure they won't. My ma will be there, and she won't let them kill Grace. If we go hunting, it breaks our contract with the charity, you see."

Isabelle nodded. The website had explained that. The families had to agree not to hunt the snow leopards, or the *argali*, the wild sheep that the snow leopards lived on.

"We'll lose a lot of money if we break the contract, and they won't buy our crafts any more." Odval looked up anxiously at Isabelle. "But everyone's so angry about the goats. I don't know whether they'll just decide to do it anyway. I don't know how to stop them," she added with a gulp.

She led Isabelle inside and back over to the painted wooden bed they'd slept in. Then she hurried to help her mother, heating a great pan of what Isabelle thought was tea, although it didn't smell quite like the tea at home. The stove in the middle of the room was for cooking on, she thought, not just for warmth.

Isabelle shrank back into the corner of the bed as several men and women came into the *ger*. She knew only Odval could see her, but when the two women sat down on the bed, she wondered if they would notice there was a girl curled up behind them. But they were fussing over the baby that one of them was carrying, wrapped up tightly in a furry hat and blankets.

The beds were like sofas in the daytime, Isabelle realized, the covers pulled tight, and cushions laid against the tall painted side of the bed. The men sat over on the other side of the *ger*, and Odval and her mother went round handing out cups of tea, pieces of white cheese and little dumplings.

It sounded as though the argument about the snow leopard had already started on the way there.

"We have to get rid of it," one of the men said firmly, taking off his coat – not a *deel*, Isabelle noticed, but a warm padded anorak like her dad might wear. "What if it comes back? They kill for pleasure, you know. It'll go mad in the sheep pens next – it could kill the lot."

"We can't, Erdene," another man said, shaking his head. From the way Odval looked gratefully at him as she handed him the cup of tea, Isabelle guessed he was her father. "You know that would break our contract. We need that money."

The two women in front of Isabelle murmured in agreement, but a younger man leaned forward eagerly. "Who's going to tell?" he broke in. He was hardly more than a boy, Isabelle realized, and another boy squashed up next to him nodded fiercely. She recognized them from the photograph – Odval's brothers.

Odval's father glared at them, and they looked down, muttering. Isabelle smiled to herself.

"So what do you say we should do, Yul?" one of the other men demanded. "Just leave that beast to kill all our stock? You know we can't afford it. Not if we have another winter like last year, another *dzud*."

"Guard the herd better, until the creature gives up and goes away. We'll set a watch, not just leave it to the dogs," Odval's father suggested.

Odval's mother sat down with the other two women, and Odval came to curl up next to Isabelle and whispered, "The *dzud* is a terrible hard winter. The white death, we call it. Last year many of our herd died."

The men went on arguing back and

forth for a while, until at last Odval's father shook his head. "We can't hunt the snow leopard. You know we can't. We rely on the money from the handicrafts." He looked over at Odval's mother, and she nodded. "We can't risk losing it. Besides, the creatures are…" He stopped, searching for a word. "Unnatural. Don't you remember the story? It's bad luck to kill one."

The other men shifted and sighed uncomfortably as he went on. "One of my cousins shot a snow leopard and wounded it, and it went to ground, hiding in a cave up in the mountains. He watched for it for three days and he heard it wail, like a ghost. Then at last it was silent. My cousin went back to his *ger*, triumphant, and then the message came, from the monastery where his son was studying. The boy had been taken ill. He'd lain on his bed crying out for three days, and then he died."

"That's just superstition," muttered the taller of Odval's brothers, and the other nodded. But he looked sideways as he did it, as though he wasn't quite sure. The other men muttered and frowned and seemed to agree with Yul. They finished their tea, and went back out, talking about mending a crumbling wall on the sheep pen.

Isabelle looked round at Odval. "That sounded hopeful," she whispered.

"Yes, if the snow leopard doesn't steal from us again." Odval nodded and got up, going to fetch a plate of food, which she brought back to share with Isabelle. "Are you hungry? There's some curds left, and cheese. It's good, you should try it."

Isabelle nibbled
on a piece of
curd, not
quite sure
what it
was. But it
tasted sweet,
and milky,
and she was
very hungry.

"It's definitely only you that knows where the snow leopards' den is?" she asked Odval quietly.

Odval glanced over at her mother, who was busy by the stove, and whispered back, "Yes. But my brothers and my uncle could find it maybe, if they tried. Snow leopards leave prints in the snow, and they scratch rocks. They could track her.

Or make a trap and bait it with food. I'm not sure I trust Sukhe and Altan to do as my pa says."

Isabelle shuddered. "Perhaps we should go back to the cave and keep watch?"

Odval nodded, but then she made a face. "I can't. My ma needs help with the felt animals. And I have to do my schoolwork."

"There's a school here?" Isabelle said.

"No, quite far away in the town. Next year, when I'm bigger, I'll have to go and stay in the dormitory by the school."

"By yourself?" Isabelle looked at Odval sympathetically. "Won't that be strange?"

But Odval looked surprised. "No. Sukhe and Altan loved it. There'll be other girls to talk to. And a proper teacher! Here I just have to study by myself. But I still have to get the work done; I can't go up the mountain now." She stood and pulled a couple of workbooks from a drawer in the wooden bed. "I wish I could…" she added, looking anxiously at the door of the *ger*.

Isabelle chewed her bottom lip. What if Sukhe and Altan did try and track Grace? She slipped off the bed and turned determinedly to look at Odval.

"Could you tear a bit of paper off the corner of the book? If you draw me a map showing how to get to the den, I can go and make sure that they're all right."

Odval nodded eagerly. "Would you be all right, climbing up on your own?"

"Yes," Isabelle told her firmly. She wasn't sure that she would be at all, but the snow leopard and her cubs were so precious, she couldn't bear to think of someone hurting them. "If anyone comes too close to the den, what should I do?"

Odval frowned. "Shout, I suppose. Frighten the snow leopards away." She smiled. "It's better for you to do it. My uncle or my brothers wouldn't hear you, would they?"

Isabelle giggled. "No, I suppose not. They'd just think that the snow leopards heard them coming." She gave Odval a hug and felt the girl stiffen in surprise, and then hug her back hard. *She must be lonely*, Isabelle decided, *with two brothers so much older, and no school to go to.* There didn't seem to be any other children here for her to be friends with, only the baby. Perhaps that was why she had gone off on her own so much. She had found the snow leopards to love.

Odval scribbled her a little map, and Isabelle put her *deel* and boots back on, and a warm furry hat. Then she slipped out, opening the door when Odval's mother wasn't looking.

And she set out alone to make the trek back up the mountainside.

# CHAPTER SIX

It was much, much harder on her own. Even getting as far as the *obo*, Isabelle was breathless. By the time she got to the scree slope, she was almost ready to give up, and go back and tell Odval that she couldn't do it – they'd just have to go together later. Her arms ached from hauling herself up the grassy climb between the boulders, and she'd scratched her cold-numbed hands on a sharp ridge of stone under the snow. Now that she was out here, she couldn't help thinking of the snow leopard's claws and teeth, too. What if Grace was frightened and leaped at her?

But then she thought of the cubs – especially little Sky. She gritted her teeth and struggled on, picking a trail up the scree slope, pausing every other step as small pebbles tumbled past her.

At last, she came to Odval's watching place, the rocks where they had sat before, with a clear view up to the snow leopards' cave.

All was silent, and for a moment Isabelle wondered if they were sleeping. But even though she couldn't hear the leopards, Isabelle was almost sure they were there – watching her. She sat still, hardly daring to breathe, her hands tucked tightly inside her long sleeves. Finally, the two cubs came cautiously nosing out of the cave, slinking around the rocks, trying to be as careful and graceful as their mother.

*Perhaps she's left them to go hunting,* Isabelle thought, hoping the leopard wouldn't have been daring enough to go back to the herders' camp in the daylight.

The larger cub sniffed the freezing air and waved his club-like tail. He forgot about being sensible and graceful. Instead he bounced on his fat paws and sprang at his sister. He rolled her over and over, and Isabelle bit her lip, wanting to go and pull them apart. Sky was so little! But then the smaller cub wriggled out of her brother's hold. She leaped up on to a ledge above, bounding down and landing on his back. The fight looked so fierce that Isabelle gasped, wondering if they were going to hurt each other. But even though they were growling and hissing, it all seemed to be a game. The two cubs rolled and wrestled for a minute or so, and then they flopped down side by side, panting and licking at each other's ears.

Isabelle flinched as she heard a scuffling noise further down the mountainside. Had someone tracked the snow leopards to their den? Or worse, had she *led* someone to the den? Isabelle pressed her hand against her mouth, panicked. Could she even be tracked if she wasn't actually here? It was so confusing.

But then she forgot the strange dream-life she was leading, as she saw the mother snow leopard bounding up the mountainside in great leaps. Isabelle gazed, spellbound, as the cat's strong back legs sent her surging forward. How did she cling on like that? Isabelle thought of her own slow, difficult ascent of the rocky paths and sighed. It was as though the snow leopard was made for this mountain. Isabelle could even see how her camouflage worked, as she stopped and crouched for a leap. Her dappled spots seemed to be part of the shadow-pattern of the rocks and snow – when she wasn't moving, she was almost impossible to see.

She wasn't carrying anything in her mouth, Isabelle saw, as Grace bounded up on to the ledge, so close that Isabelle could almost have reached out to touch the long fur fringing her belly. She hadn't managed to catch anything, so the cubs would have to go hungry.

They jumped up as they saw their mother coming, running along the ledge towards her eagerly. Isabelle wasn't sure if she was imagining that they looked hopeful, and then disappointed... She wondered how long it was since they had all eaten. What if they were so hungry that Grace was tempted to go back to the easy pickings in the animal pens, just to feed her children?

Grace shook herself and yawned, then led her babies into the cave. It looked to

Isabelle as though they were going to curl up and sleep for the day. Odval had said that they were most active at dawn and dusk. Should she stay and keep watching for any hunters? Isabelle wrapped her arms tightly around her middle and pulled the furry hat that Odval had given her down further over her ears. It was so cold, even where she was sheltered from the biting wind in between the rocks. She couldn't stay here for much longer, she realized. She would freeze. Already she could hardly feel her fingers.

Slowly, carefully, she began to stumble back towards the camp, clenching and unclenching her frozen hands to try and draw the feeling back into them. She hesitated at the top of the scree slope, not wanting to take the first step on to those shifting stones. Without

Odval to help steady her, how was she
going to get down? Isabelle turned herself
sideways, and began to inch downwards. She
was almost back to the path when her ankle
seemed to twist underneath her and
she skidded horribly fast. She
tried to scrabble at
the rocks and
catch herself,
but they slid
out from
under her
hands, and
she rolled
and tumbled
down to the path, breathless and gasping.

Isabelle lay for a moment, unsure how
badly she was hurt. She had been so lucky
not to have rolled further – there was a

steep drop to the side of the path, and she could have fallen all the way down. She sat up slowly. Her hands were sore – and she had a feeling that they might hurt more when they weren't so cold – but apart from that, she seemed miraculously unharmed. Isabelle let out a shaky sigh of relief, and then giggled. She was down, and safe, and in a few minutes she would be back with Odval. She could tell her that Grace and the cubs were well, hidden away in their den. But the snow leopards hadn't eaten – which meant that at dusk, when she went out hunting again for her family, Grace would be hungrier and more daring than ever…

Isabelle spent the rest of the morning watching Odval and her mother making tiny, beautiful objects from the felted wool. It seemed amazing that they were using wool that had come from their own sheep and goats. They didn't just make Christmas decorations, either. Odval was stitching a tiny pair of slippers for a baby – they were gorgeous, a rich purple colour, with white snowflakes embroidered on to the front. But her mum didn't let her help for long – she sent Odval back to do her schoolwork and started to spin yarn on a spinning wheel.

"Is that from your sheep, too?" Isabelle whispered, looking at the tawny clumps.

"No, that's camel hair," Odval told her, and Isabelle stared.

"You can shear a *camel*?" she squeaked in surprise. She couldn't imagine a camel standing still to let anyone cut its hair.

"Mmm-hmm. Most of it just falls out, though, and we gather it up. Camels are really difficult to shear – you have to tip them over with ropes and then sit on them." Odval giggled. "It takes a lot of people to sit on a camel. Ma spins the hair, and we sell it for people to knit with. You have to get a lot of muck out of it first, though. It's always full of bits of straw and dirt."

Odval's father and brothers came back to the *ger* for a midday meal, and afterwards Sukhe and Altan asked to borrow their father's gun, so they could go hunting for marmots. Isabelle saw Odval watching them, with a strange look on her face.

"What is it? Do you think they're not really going after marmots?" Isabelle asked. She wasn't sure what a marmot was, but she decided not to ask.

"I don't know," Odval muttered. "They keep smirking at each other. I'm supposed to gather up the sheep dung to dry, to make *khurgul* to burn in the stove. If you help me, we could get it done quickly and go after them, couldn't we?"

Isabelle swallowed. *Gathering sheep poo? Really?* But she nodded. After watching the cubs and their mother that morning, she knew that she would do anything to keep them safe. "It's just grass," she muttered to herself. "Grass that's been all the way through a sheep, that's all." And she'd seen it burning, she thought. The *ger* had been quite warm, the stove obviously kept burning low all through the night. The *khurgul* hadn't smelled bad.

Odval's father and some of the other men had taken the sheep back out to pasture again. Odval had explained that they knew the best places, close to the streams, and where it was windy enough to blow the snow off the grasses, but not too exposed. On really bad days, the sheep would stay in their pen and be fed on the dried grass. They herded the sheep on horseback and Uncle Erdene rode his motorbike.

The two girls went into the pen and used spades to gather up the dung that the sheep had left behind, stacking it to dry so it could then be made into blocks for burning. They watched Sukhe and Altan disappear off up a different path to the one they'd used that morning, and Odval wrinkled her nose worriedly and worked even faster. The boys had only been gone for a few minutes when Odval looked at the piles of dung and nodded. "That's good enough. Now we can go after Sukhe and Altan. If we take one of the horses, we can catch them up."

"But a horse won't be able to go up the side of the mountain, will it?" Isabelle said.

"They went that way," Odval explained, pointing, "towards the old mine works. It's been abandoned for ages, but the path is quite flat, easy enough for a horse. If it gets too steep, we'll tie him up somewhere sheltered and leave him till we come back."

Isabelle watched while Odval saddled up the iron-grey horse. She knew that he didn't have a name, but the mottled dark pattern on his flanks was so like dark storm clouds that she decided to call him

Cloud, just to herself.

Cloud seemed to be very good-natured, and stood calmly while Odval adjusted his saddle and bridle. He didn't object to the two of them on his back, either, or all the hopping about as Odval hauled Isabelle up behind her. He just peered round at her curiously and snorted. Isabelle smiled to herself, imagining what Daisy would think if she could see her now. She'd never ridden like this before. On holiday she'd only been trail-riding, and then always on a very quiet pony in a long string of other riders. This felt like real riding, even if she was holding on to Odval.

Odval walked Cloud cautiously, pulling him up at every turn along the path, to make sure that her brothers weren't somewhere just ahead.

After a few minutes, Isabelle tugged her arm. "I can hear voices!"

"Yes, me too," Odval agreed. The girls slipped down from Cloud, and Odval looped his reins around a bush. Isabelle realized in surprise that the stunted little bush was the biggest plant that she had seen up here. There were no trees at all.

Leaving Cloud nibbling at the leaves, the two girls crept on down the path, and eventually stopped by a rocky outcrop so they could spy on Sukhe and Altan. The boys were standing looking down at something and talking to each other. The gun was propped up against some rocks.

"Is it deep enough?" Altan muttered.

"I reckon so. But we need to smooth out the sides."

"What are they looking at?" Isabelle whispered.

"The old mine pit," Odval whispered back. "It was a copper mine, but it never worked very well. There wasn't much copper, and it was too hard to get what they did mine back to the city. So they never dug all that deep. It's just a hole. People still try and dig in it every so often, but it never comes to much." She scowled. "I know what they're doing. It's a trap. They're going to try and use it to trap Grace."

"Even after what your pa said?"

Odval nodded. "They want to show off. They want to be the big men who catch the snow leopard." She sighed.

They watched as the two boys fetched flat stones from around the path and lugged them to the edge of the pit. Then they climbed down with a spade, and all the girls could see was them occasionally climbing up to fetch a stone, cursing at how heavy they were.

"Are they trying to stop her climbing out?" Isabelle asked doubtfully.

"They must be." Odval shook her head and gave Isabelle a hopeful look. "I think they're trying to make the sides slope, so she can't scramble up. It won't work, will it? She's much too good at climbing to get caught in something like that."

"She went straight up the mountainside

when I was watching her this morning," Isabelle agreed. "I don't see how a pit could hold her, not unless it's really deep. They wouldn't be able to give it sheer sides, would they? And why would Grace go in it, anyway? Are they going to bait it with something?"

"Meat." Odval nodded. "I bet they've taken some of the meat from the goats that were killed. The cold froze it, so it's stored outside one of the *ger*s." She laughed, rather sadly. "Poor Grace, she'll get her goat's meat after all."

"But do you think she'll come here? We aren't all that close to her den, are we?"

Odval looked past the mine pit, and then back down the path, frowning a little as though she was measuring in her head. "Actually, we are. If we went further along this path, you'd see it turns and goes steeper up the mountain. It's longer, but it joins on to the path we used to get to the den. It would be no distance at all for Grace. My pa said that snow leopards can range for miles and miles in just one night when they haven't got cubs to watch." She glanced angrily back at the pit. "I don't know how they worked it out – it was probably just luck – but they've picked a really good place."

"Do you think you should tell your pa?" Isabelle suggested. "He'd stop them, wouldn't he?"

"How can I?" Odval muttered. "Then I'd have to tell him that I know there's a snow leopard, and I've been disappearing off to watch her for months. My ma and pa would be so upset with me. I'm not supposed to go that far away from the camp. I bet they'd never let me go anywhere on my own ever again." Her eyes widened. "They might even say they can't trust me to go to school! Besides, Sukhe is the eldest and he's really good at working with the herds. Pa thinks he's sensible. He'd just deny it. And we can hardly prove anything, can we? It's just a hole!"

"I suppose so," Isabelle agreed gloomily. "So we'll just have to hope that if Grace does jump into it, she can scramble out again." She thought of Grace bounding past her, and she was almost sure that no pit could hold her. But only almost.

"We have to do something," Isabelle murmured, watching the boys and biting angrily at her lip. "We can't let them trap her, it's too cruel..." She remembered all the snow leopard facts she'd read, how few of them there were left. They had to help, she and Odval.

"Maybe that's why I'm here," Isabelle whispered to herself, too quietly for Odval to hear. She knew that she wasn't really an imaginary friend – but she still didn't know what she *was*. This strange world felt far too real to be a dream. But Isabelle was sure of one thing – she had to save Grace and the cubs.

# CHAPTER
# SEVEN

"I've been thinking," Isabelle said, as she helped Odval untack Cloud and turn him back into his stall. "Could we take the bait out of the trap? So they don't catch her?"

Odval smiled at her delightedly. "I didn't think of that!" She glanced up at the sky. "But we'd have to be quick – it'll be dark really soon." Then her face fell. "If they've put the meat right at the bottom of the pit, I'm not sure we can get down there. It's really steep."

"We'd need a ladder," Isabelle suggested. "Have you got one?"

"A stepladder, for helping put the *ger* canvas up, that's all... It would wobble around too much."

"The *ger*!" Isabelle caught Odval's hands. "Yes! There are spare bits of the wood framework, aren't there? I saw them by the sheep pen."

"The *khana*? Yes, there are spares in case a panel breaks."

"Well, aren't they just like a ladder? I could get my feet into those holes." She smiled, remembering the time she'd climbed her mum's garden trellis to rescue a stuck tennis ball.

Odval nodded. "We could try, anyway. Look, the boys are back."

Altan and Sukhe were sauntering through the camp, dangling a sad bundle of fur that Isabelle supposed was a marmot. It looked a bit like an otter with no tail, and she glanced away, shuddering. Still, in a winter like this, she knew Odval's family would be glad of it – both the meat and the fur.

Sukhe picked up Odval and twirled her round, making her giggle in spite of herself.

"What are you so happy about?" she panted, when he finally put her down. Then she wobbled, dizzy, and Altan caught her hands to steady her.

Isabelle watched them, frowning to herself. Even though the boys were hunters – they'd killed the poor marmot, and they wanted to kill Grace – they clearly adored their little sister. And Odval loved them back. No wonder this was difficult for her.

Sukhe patted Odval's cheek. "Nothing you need to know about. We're just looking after you, that's all. Looking after everyone," he added seriously.

"You should be back inside soon, Odval," Altan called, as they headed back to the *ger*. "It's getting dark."

"I know." Odval nodded, and the two girls watched the boys walk away.

"Should we go now?" Isabelle suggested. "Before your ma comes out looking for you?"

Odval nodded, running over to the

canvas-covered pile by the sheep pen. "My pa never throws anything away," she explained to Isabelle. "He reckons all of this will come in useful one day." She lifted up an old tyre and the two girls pulled out a tall wooden lattice, about two metres long.

It was stronger than the trellis, Isabelle thought. She'd definitely be able to climb it, if they could stretch it out and stand it up straight.

The girls slipped and scrambled back up to the path, sliding on the frozen grass as they tried to hurry. It was already starting to get dark and blue shadows were emerging across the snow-scattered grasslands. The path to the mine was eerie in the fading light, and Isabelle felt her stomach turn over as they peered down into the pit for the first time. Odval had said it wasn't very deep – but it looked almost bottomless, filled with shadows.

"It must be all right to climb down into," Isabelle said shakily. "The miners had to go down, didn't they?"

Odval nodded uncertainly. "I suppose. The meat's there, look." She pointed to a ledge, about three metres down. Isabelle could see a joint of meat, lying on the rock.

"I think it's long enough," Odval murmured, as they pulled at the lattice to stretch it out. "Are you sure you don't want me to do it, though?"

Isabelle shook her head. "You hold it tight at the top." She swallowed, as they fed the lattice down into the hole. It looked so wobbly. "We can rest it on the ledge."

Odval untied the sash from her *deel* and threaded it through a couple of squares of the lattice, tying the ends into a knot and wrapping her arms through it. "I can hold it lower down like this," she explained. "It's going to be tricky for you to reach the meat."

"Ready?" Isabelle asked, pushing back her sleeves and wincing at the freezing air on her scratched hands. It was the sideways step from the edge of the pit on to the ladder that would be the worst bit, she thought, trying to take a deep breath. It felt like there was something in her throat, the air didn't seem to be going in properly. She stepped down on to a little ledge, just below the edge of the pit, and reached her foot sideways, feeling for a foothold. For a panicky moment there was nothing there, and then her foot found the trellis.

"One foot after the other," Isabelle whispered to herself, trying to ignore the way the slats flexed and shook under her weight. It seemed to take a very long time to get down to the ledge.

Back at home, Isabelle would have hated to pick up a joint of meat – but now she didn't have time to fuss. She just grabbed it, tucking the frozen lump into the pocket made by the double front of the *deel*. *At least it's frozen*, she thought. *I won't get covered in meaty bits, ugh…* Then she smiled, thinking of the snow leopards. They would think the meaty bits were delicious. And Odval had said how close the den was.

"Can we take it to Grace and the cubs?" she gasped, as Odval hauled her out over the edge.

Odval pulled up the wooden frame and nodded. "Good idea. We can hide the *khana* here – in case we have to raid the trap again."

Isabelle tried to smile. She really hoped

that they wouldn't. Odval hugged her. "Next time I'll climb. You were so brave. I can't believe I thought you weren't real. I thought I'd dreamed you up, but I can't have done, can I?"

"I don't know," Isabelle whispered, held tightly in her friend's arms.

"Sarangerel! Wake up!"

Isabelle groaned and turned over. It couldn't be time for school.

"Wake up!"

Isabelle opened her eyes to see Odval peering down at her. She was still here, in the *ger*!

In her head, she had said goodbye to Odval and the snow leopards the night before, when they'd left the joint of meat on the ledge below the snow leopard cave, and come back to the *ger* for supper and sleep. Isabelle had been sure that she would wake up in her own bed in the morning, and she would never see them again. For a moment, she didn't know whether to be disappointed or not. But then Odval shook her desperately, and she forgot her home and the strangeness of the dream. It was all too real.

"Sukhe and Altan are going out somewhere!" Odval hissed. "Put on your boots, we have to follow them. We need to see what they do when they find the meat's gone."

Isabelle shivered. She didn't really feel like going out into the freezing dark. "I suppose…" she murmured. "Perhaps they'll just give up," she added hopefully.

She wrapped the *deel* round herself, yawning hugely, and stumbled to the door. Odval grabbed some leftover dumplings and cheese from the night before, and stuffed them into a bag. Then they dashed out into the eerie pre-dawn light of the morning. The sky was stacked with heavy clouds, gathering over the mountains.

"Ugh, it's going to snow," Odval muttered, glancing up at the clouds. "It might be heavy. Look, there they are."

Isabelle could see the light of the boys' torches – it looked like they'd just been to get some more meat from the store stacked by the side of the *ger*. "More?" she whispered to Odval, as they hurried along behind the boys, trying to step quietly. She felt Odval shrug beside her.

"I still reckon it must have been an

eagle," Altan said. He wasn't bothering to whisper. "Good thing we sneaked out to check."

"Or that snow leopard got in and managed to climb out again. I told you it wasn't deep enough! I hope the beast hasn't done it again. Ma is going to notice this much meat disappearing as it is."

Isabelle caught Odval's sleeve, and the two girls stopped, clutching each other in horror. Sukhe and Altan had gone back and refilled the trap after everyone had gone to bed! Isabelle's frightening climb down the side of the pit had been for nothing.

"I never thought they'd do that," Odval whispered. "Sarangerel, if they put more bait down, they might have trapped Grace after all!"

The two girls ran up the path, hand in hand, hearts thudding. Isabelle wished they could go faster, but they couldn't turn on Odval's torch in case the boys looked back. Sukhe and Altan were drawing ahead already. What if they were too late, and Grace was trapped? What would the boys do to her?

"Slow down, we're almost there," Odval whispered, putting out a hand to stop Isabelle. "Can you hear them?"

Isabelle nodded grimly. Odval's brothers were so excited they were practically shouting. As they peered around the rock wall, the girls could see them jumping about and hugging each other on the edge of the path. It was getting lighter, but snow was starting to fall, Isabelle realized vaguely – she could just about make out the boys through a mist of snowflakes. At home she would have dashed outside to dance around, but now she didn't even care. It didn't matter. Only Grace mattered.

"We caught it – the ghost of the mountain!" Sukhe crowed. "No more goat-stealing for you!"

"I can't believe we trapped the beast!" Altan threw an arm round his brother's shoulders, and the two girls exchanged miserable looks.

"Why didn't she jump out?" Isabelle whispered. "I was sure she'd be able to."

"Maybe she hurt herself?" Odval shook her head. "I don't understand either. But she often goes out hunting at dawn. Maybe she's only just gone into the pit after the meat. If she heard the boys coming, she'd probably just huddle down at the bottom of it... Oh, that would be so cruel, such bad luck!"

"She really wouldn't jump out while they're watching?"

"No, I don't think so. Snow leopards are so shy. They never attack people. I was the only person in my family who'd seen one until today! She's probably trying to hide and wait until they go..."

"What are they going to do to her?" Isabelle peered out again, trying to hear what the boys were discussing.

"I'll go and fetch it. It's beside his bed," Altan said eagerly, and Sukhe nodded.

"Pa's gun!" Odval whispered in horror, pushing Isabelle back into the shadow of the pile of rocks as Altan hurried past. "He's going to get the gun. They'll shoot her!"

"No!" Isabelle shook her head, her eyes terrified. "We can't let them."

"We'll have to follow Altan and tell Pa," Odval decided. "Keep quiet – we don't want Sukhe to hear us."

But it was almost impossible to tread too loudly now, Isabelle realized, as they crept out on to the path again. The snow was falling so thickly that the path was covered in a couple of centimetres of fresh snow already. And it was getting worse. Odval had to switch on her torch just to see where they were going. The light had changed to a ghostly blue, and the snowflakes whirled around them in a silent swarm.

"I can't see…" Isabelle admitted to
Odval after a few minutes of walking.

"Nor can I…" Odval sounded worried
– scared almost – and Isabelle felt blindly
for her hand. So much here was strange
that she had thought Odval would know
what to do. The Mongolian girl would be

able to see in the snow, somehow. But her face looked frightened, as Isabelle peered at her through the rising storm. The torch beam was doing nothing, it was just a faint yellowish gleam in front of them. The wind had picked up and it howled, whirling the snow around them.

"We just have to keep going," Odval shouted. "We'll find the way down off this path to the gers soon. Altan!" she called suddenly. "Altan, help!" But there was no answer. "I don't think he can hear us," she muttered. Then, after a few more minutes, she tugged on Isabelle's hand. "We've gone too far... We should have found the path down by now."

"Where are we?" Isabelle gasped, trying not to sound panicky. The snow was settling on her face, and it was starting to freeze painfully around her nose and eyes.

"I don't know," Odval admitted. "Unless... What's that noise?"

Isabelle strained to hear. There was a rustling, snapping sound just ahead. It did sound oddly familiar. "I don't know... Oh! The *obo*!" It was the plastic streamers tied on to the stones, snapping and jerking in the fierce wind.

"If we follow this path, we'll come to the snow leopards' den," Odval shouted back against the wind. "We have to get out of this storm – it's dangerous. We can shelter in the cave. We'll need to climb up on to the ledge – follow me." She pulled Isabelle after her, and they trudged on, picking their way around the rocks that loomed up suddenly in the failing torchlight.

"Stay against the rock wall!" Odval cried suddenly, lurching towards Isabelle. "There's a drop – I almost slipped."

Isabelle grabbed her, pulling Odval back flat against the rock. "Are you all right?"

"Yes!" Odval sobbed out. "We – we must be close to the ledge under the cave." The screaming wind snatched away the snow for a moment, like a hand pulling aside a curtain. Isabelle shuddered as she looked down at the narrow ledge they were standing on and pressed her back against the side of the mountain. But Odval pointed ahead. "Look! The rocks where we sat. Come on!"

They had never climbed up on to the ledge before, not wanting to scare the snow leopards. Isabelle had wanted to go closer for a better look, but Odval had explained that if they got too close, Grace might even abandon her den. But it wasn't that steep – there were crevices and ledges in the rock that meant the girls could shove and haul each other up close to the cave, even in the snow storm.

Isabelle hesitated at the dark opening – should they go in? What about the cubs?

"Come on, Sarangerel," Odval muttered. "If we stay out here, we'll freeze. I mean it."

# CHAPTER
# EIGHT

"I can see them," Isabelle said suddenly. The two cubs were peering at the girls out of the darkness of the den and they flinched away, hissing, as Odval swung the torchbeam across the cave. It was long and narrow – it looked almost as if two rocks had squashed together. It didn't feel very cosy, but at least it was out of the wind and snow. Isabelle hated to break into the cubs' safe home – but Odval was right, it was dangerously cold for the two girls outside.

"We saw your mother," she whispered to the cubs. "We helped her, but she still got caught. She'll be back soon…" She looked over at Odval, her eyes filling with tears. Would Grace ever return home to her babies? "We'll look after you…" she promised. "Somehow." *Even if your mother never comes back*, she added to herself.

"We've got food," Odval said, as they slipped inside the cave, curling up against the wall as far away from the cubs as they could. The snow leopards lay pressed against the opposite wall, watching them anxiously. "We could feed them. They can't have had much of that meat last night, and they hadn't eaten for a while before that – you said Grace didn't bring anything back yesterday. I bet they're hungry." Odval pulled the bag of food out from the front of her *deel* and opened it up, resting the torch on a rock so she could see what she was doing.

Shadow sat up at once, making a low noise in his throat, a curious sort of yowling. He was obviously hungry. He padded cautiously towards them, stopping an arm's length away and eyeing the meat dumpling that Odval had broken open. She tossed it to him gently, so that it fell just in front of his paws, and he sniffed at it for a moment. Then he gave the girls one last careful glance and gobbled down the treat in one mouthful.

"What about your sister?" Isabelle murmured, laughing as he came towards them, sniffing eagerly at Odval's hands and the bag. But Sky stayed pressed against the far wall, and Isabelle thought she was trembling.

"Throw some towards her," she suggested to Odval, and Odval tried, but

Shadow whipped round and pounced on the food before his sister could get near.

Odval looked out at the snow, which seemed to be falling more and more thickly. "We'd better save the rest for the moment," she decided, tucking the bag behind her. "We don't know how long we'll all be here. And we might need some food, too. Sometimes a blizzard can go on for a long time. Last winter, there was a storm that went on for two days. My ma and pa just about managed to get out and feed the animals, but that was all."

Isabelle nodded. She leaned against Odval, suddenly weary. They were safer now that they were out of the storm, but the den was freezing. She could see her breath, smoky and white in front of her face. She shuddered as the wind screamed by outside. And poor Grace was still trapped. *What will Odval's parents think?* she wondered suddenly. *They'll wake up and find her gone. Maybe they have already. Her and Sukhe. But Altan should be back by now. He'll know where Sukhe is, I suppose.*

She glanced round, about to ask Odval if her parents would go and look for her – but Odval was asleep, worn out by their terrifying climb.

Shadow was watching them, clearly hoping for more food. He edged closer and closer, so that he was almost touching Odval's feet.

"Will you warm us up?" Isabelle whispered, and the little snow leopard sniffed at their boots hopefully, as if he thought they might be food. Disappointed, he slumped down, with his muzzle resting on Odval's boot. He wriggled and turned himself round a few times, padding at Odval to make her more comfortable, just like Gran's cat did. Then he wrapped his thick tail around his face like a warm scarf and closed his eyes. Isabelle smiled delightedly – but then she looked back over at Sky.

Was she a little closer than she'd been before? Isabelle looked away, not wanting to scare her off.

*What about* my *mum and dad?* she thought to herself. *Are they worried, too? Am I actually here, and not at home? I thought it was just a dream, but it isn't, it can't be. It's gone on too long. It's too real. How am I going to get home?* She reached out a cautious hand to pat Shadow's rough head.

"I don't know what's going to happen," she whispered, glancing across the cave at Sky. The little grey cub stared back at her, her eyes gleaming in the faint torchlight. "What are we going to do?" Isabelle felt her voice wobble, and she pressed her hands over her eyes. Now that Odval was asleep, she felt so much more alone – and frightened. What if they couldn't save Grace? What if they never found their way down the mountain? She caught her breath, trying to stop herself from crying.

There was a faint scuffling noise, and Isabelle peered through her fingers, not moving. Sky was coming! "Are you trying to make me feel better?" Isabelle whispered. "Could you hear me crying?"

The little cub padded slowly across the cave and Isabelle held her breath. The cub sat down next to her brother and stared, her blue eyes glowing in the torchlight.

"I'm supposed to be looking after you," Isabelle said, her voice still shaking. "That's why we came... But now it feels like you're worrying about me."

Sky gazed into her eyes, and made a snuffling sound, blowing out through her nostrils. Then she rubbed the side of her face against Isabelle's foot.

"Do you want some food?" Isabelle whispered, reaching behind Odval for the bag. "Here, look." She pulled out a dumpling and the cub leaned forward hopefully. Isabelle was about to throw it for her, when she daintily seized it out of her hand – the same with the next. And then she lay down next to the girls, resting her head in Isabelle's lap.

Isabelle ran her hand over Sky's ears and yawned. She'd been half asleep, even though it was daytime. There was something about Sky snoozing on top of her that had made her sleepy, too. She stretched a little, wondering how much time had passed and realizing how stiff she was, how much everything ached. Shadow was at the entrance to the den, looking out. He glanced round as he heard Isabelle move.

"It's stopped snowing!" she gasped, looking at the patch of clear sky showing in the cave mouth. "Odval, wake up. It's stopped. We can go back."

Odval stretched wearily and Sky sat up with a huge cat-yawn, showing all her white teeth. "I should go home – my parents…" She made a face. "They'll be so worried. The storm must have lasted a couple of hours, I think."

Isabelle nodded. "But we need to check the pit, as well, and see if Grace is still there." She frowned. "I could do that – I'm sure I can find the way. You'd better go straight back."

"No, I'm coming with you!" Odval shook her head firmly. "A few more minutes won't make much difference. I bet Sukhe didn't stay on guard through the storm; he must have gone home, too. Let's hope Grace climbed out."

"But wouldn't she have returned to her cubs?" Isabelle reached out to stroke Sky, and then glanced worriedly at Shadow, waiting at the cave entrance. "Shadow's looking for her, I think."

"Perhaps she couldn't come back?" Odval shrugged helplessly. "We have to go and see. Maybe we can rescue her."

Isabelle nodded and gently pushed Sky away. "Shall we leave them the last of the food?" She pulled out the bag and opened it up, getting out the sheep's milk cheese that was left and piling it in the middle of the cave. Both cubs ran to sniff at it, as the girls stood at the opening.

"We'll see you soon," Odval promised, as they stepped out on to the snowy ledge and began to climb down carefully.

As Isabelle glanced back up from the ledge below, she saw that both cubs had abandoned the food and were standing in the den entrance, gazing worriedly after them.

"It'll be all right," Isabelle whispered. "She'll come home." Inside the long sleeve of her *deel*, she crossed her fingers, pleading with all the spirits of the mountain. She wasn't sure she believed in them, but Odval did. "Bring her back to them," she begged, as she followed Odval down the path.

"She *is* still down there!" Isabelle gasped, pointing to the heap of huddled fur in the corner of the pit. "Oh, she must be hurt. Maybe she injured herself when she jumped in?"

The snow leopard looked up at them and hissed. She stood up – was she limping a little? Isabelle wasn't quite sure. She couldn't see a wound.

"I can't see Sukhe anywhere," Odval said. "He must have gone back to the *ger*. We have to get her out of here before he returns."

"If we put the *khana* back down there, would she climb up it?" Isabelle suggested.

Odval sighed. "Maybe – it's got to be worth a try, anyway. I can't see any other way of getting her out."

They had to dig away a thick covering of snow over the rocks where they'd hidden the wooden lattice, but at last they pulled it out. They stood at the edge of the pit, wrenching at the rawhide strips that tied it all together. They were stiff with cold, and Isabelle wanted to scream with frustration. Sukhe and Altan could be back any moment. "There!" she gasped, as the lattice finally opened out.

Cautiously, the girls leaned over the edge, lowering the wooden frame down. They didn't want to hit Grace.

The snow leopard skulked away to the other side of the pit. "She is limping, I think," Odval said. "I hope she can still get up this... Here, untie your sash and I'll take off mine – we can use them to hold the frame up. She won't climb past us if we're holding on to the wood."

They stood a couple of steps away,

gripping the ends of the sashes and hoping.

Nothing happened for so many long moments, and then there was a scuffling and a scraping and a sudden weight dragging on their arms. Isabelle gasped and leaned back as the snow leopard came leaping up out of the trap, bounding past them in a blur of grey, and vanishing up the path, towards her babies.

The two girls watched her go, open-mouthed, and then Odval threw her arms around Isabelle and smiled – a wide grin of pure happiness. "We did it!" She looked back up the path and gave a tiny sigh.

"She'll leave here now, you know. She won't stay this close to the *gers*, now that she's been so scared. She'll be able to smell us in the den, too. So I probably won't see her again. But it means she'll be safe, far away from our *gers*! She was my secret, for so long…" Odval stroked Isabelle's sleeve. "My secret, just like you."

"We rescued her, and the cubs…" Isabelle said slowly. "That's why I came, I think. Why you wished me to come, I mean."

"Are you going now, too?" Odval asked.

"I don't know… Oh, Odval, look!"

Coming back towards them down the path was the snow leopard, pacing slowly, her great tail swinging. She was favouring one front leg, just a little. And pattering after her – reaching up now and then to bat at that swinging tail – were Shadow and Sky.

"They're going to their new home," Isabelle whispered.

The two girls stepped back, pressing themselves against the rocks, as the snow leopards passed.

Grace looked up and paused, just for a second, gazing at them with her clear, greenish eyes. It was the first time Isabelle had looked into her face, and she felt as though she would never be able to forget it – the dark lines above her eyes, with delicate arches of tiny spots swooping over them. Isabelle was sure that Grace had stopped to say thank you. She padded on, and the cubs nosed at the two girls, nudging them and jumping up to press great padded paws against their legs.

Then they too frisked away after their
mother, and the snow leopards vanished
into the shadows of the mountain.

Isabelle sighed, but happily. She had a strange sense that everything was right — it was done. She turned to look at Odval and saw that her friend was smiling, but there were frosty tears on her cheeks.

"You might see her again," Isabelle whispered. "Maybe."

"But what about you? I think you'll go back to just being a dream." Odval reached out her hand, and Isabelle went to take it — but it was too far away. The icy cold was leaving the air, and the sparkling light of the snow was dimming. She couldn't reach Odval's hand, however hard she tried.

And then she found herself, still in the dim light of morning – but in her own bed, with the snow leopard decoration clutched in her hands.

Isabelle peered down at it, her heart thumping. Had she dreamed it all? She ran her fingers over the rough felt – and remembered Odval and her mother. It had seemed so real. She touched the bumps of the leopard's stitched markings and shook her head uncertainly. The little lines and spots over the eyes – just like Grace's.

"She was real," Isabelle murmured. "They all were."

"What have you asked for, Tilly?" Isabelle said, leaning over to look at her little sister's list. It was scribbly and smeared, and Isabelle thought it was probably a good thing that Tilly had been going round telling everybody what she wanted Father Christmas to bring for weeks. Mum would have to write it underneath, or something. Not even an elf would be able to understand Tilly's handwriting.

"A sledge and a dolls' house and two chocolate mice and a candy cane and new pink wellies!" Tilly chanted, and Isabelle giggled.

"What are you asking for, Isabelle?" Dad came past with a box of Christmas decorations. "I hope you two are nearly finished – we're almost ready to start decorating the tree."

Isabelle looked down at her list:
Riding lessons
*So I can ride like Odval,* she added in

her head. *I could go to the stables where Daisy goes. She said she'd come with me. I'll ask her about it at school on Monday; she was so nice...*

A furry hat

*Because it's freezing out there*, Isabelle thought, nibbling her pencil. *And Mum thinks it's going to snow any day.* Even *though I know it isn't really all that cold, not like it was back there, with Odval...* She gave a tiny sigh. It felt like a dream, but not a dream. She knew that it had been real somehow. *I wonder if Odval remembers me? I'll always remember her.* Then she smiled. She would remember, but when she went back to school, there'd be Daisy to talk to. And Odval would be going to school soon, too. Perhaps it was only now that they'd really needed each other?

A snow leopard

"A toy snow leopard?" Dad asked, frowning as he looked over her shoulder at the last thing on the list.

Isabelle grinned at him. "No, a real one. Don't worry, Dad, not as a pet. I want to sponsor one. I read about it – you can send money to a wildlife charity and they'll send you pictures. They have these special cameras set up, it's brilliant."

*And maybe one day, it'll be Grace in the photo,* Isabelle thought to herself. *Or Shadow, or little Sky. Will I recognize them, when they're all grown up?*

She would, she thought, remembering the way Sky had eaten from her hand and slept curled half in her lap – and the warm weight of the cubs' paws pressing against her at that last goodbye.

# BEHIND THE STORY...

This story began for me exactly the way it does for Isabelle. I went to Marwell Zoo in Hampshire (although I made the zoo further north in the story, and I changed the arrangement of the animals in the zoo, too). At Marwell, I saw their beautiful snow leopard, Irina. You can see Irina on Marwell's website, www.marwell.org.uk. Marwell Zoo are taking part in the European Breeding Programme for snow leopards, which means that zoos around Europe work together to increase the numbers of this endangered species.

Then I bought a Christmas decoration in the zoo shop, made by women who were living in the snow-leopards' habitat in Mongolia. The decorations use felted sheep's wool, or sometimes yak hair, from the families' flocks.

The desert area in Mongolia is gradually spreading. This means that herders are moving further into the snow-leopards' habitat, and feeding their flocks of sheep, goats, yaks and camels closer to the wild snow leopards. Because life can be very hard for the herders in Mongolia (and in the other countries where snow leopards are found) a snow leopard attacking the flocks is disastrous. A family who survive by selling the wool and meat from their animals can't afford to let a snow leopard destroy their livelihood, and may decide to hunt the snow leopard to protect them, as Sukhe and Altan do in this story.

The Snow Leopard Trust provides training and equipment for crafting Christmas decorations and other toys and ornaments, and they buy the finished products from the families making them. In return, the herder community makes a commitment not to hunt the snow leopards, and to work to protect them instead. The extra money from selling the decorations makes it possible for the herders to survive, even if a snow leopard steals from their flocks.

The money raised from selling the ornaments in the United States and Britain, and other countries, goes to conservation projects helping the snow leopards.

The World Wildlife Fund (WWF) is also working with communities in Mongolia and China to protect snow leopards. Have a look at wwf.org.uk.

You can find out lots more about the Snow Leopard Trust at www.snowleopard.org. You can buy decorations from Mongolia and can even adopt a snow leopard, just like Isabelle does. I have!

Love,

# THE SNOW BEAR

FROM BEST-SELLING AUTHOR
## HOLLY WEBB

# Collect them all!

A beautiful Christmas story,
perfect for bedtime reading

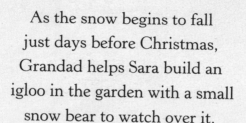

As the snow begins to fall
just days before Christmas,
Grandad helps Sara build an
igloo in the garden with a small
snow bear to watch over it.

And when Sara wakes in the
middle of the night, it looks
very different outside. She sets out
on an enchanted journey through
a world of ice, but will she ever
find her way home…

# The
# Reindeer
# Girl

FROM BEST-SELLING AUTHOR
# HOLLY WEBB

Lotta loves to hear
Great-grandmother Erika tell stories
of her childhood, herding reindeer in
the snowy north of Norway. Lotta
dreams of having such adventures, too.
Little does she know that her wish is
about to come true.

One night, just before Christmas,
Lotta wakes to find herself in the world
of her great-grandmother's stories.
And she has her very own reindeer
and calf to take care of...

# THE

# WINTER

# WOLF

FROM BEST-SELLING AUTHOR

# HOLLY WEBB

Amelia is exploring the huge, old house where her family are spending Christmas when she finds a diary hidden in the attic. It was written by a boy struggling to look after an abandoned wolf pup. Before she knows it, Amelia is transported into the wintry world of the diary.

Noah wishes he had someone to help keep a lost wolf pup safe. Then Amelia appears mysteriously one day. Together, can they find the pup's mother out in the icy wilderness?

## HOLLY WEBB

Holly Webb started out as a children's book editor, and wrote her first series for the publisher she worked for. She has been writing ever since, with over one hundred books to her name. Holly lives in Berkshire, with her husband and three young sons. Holly's pet cats are always nosying around when she is trying to type on her laptop.

For more information about Holly Webb visit:

# www.holly-webb.com